D1052767

Adventure on Thunder Island

Adventure on Thunder Island

Edna King and Jordan Wheeler

James Lorimer & Company, Publishers
Toronto, 1991

1-55028-133-X paper

1-55028-135-6 cloth

Cover illustration: C. J. Taylor

Canadian Cataloguing in Publication Data

King, Edna
Adventure on Thunder Island
(A Lorimer blue kite book)
ISBN 1-55028-135-6 (bound) ISBN 1-55028-133-X (pbk.)
1. Indians of North America - Canada - Juvenile fiction.
I. Wheeler, Jordan, 1964- . II. Title. III. Series.
PS8571.I54A65 1991 jC813'.54 C88-094860-4
PZ7.K55Ad 1991

James Lorimer & Company, Publishers
Egerton Ryerson Memorial Building
35 Britain Street
Toronto, Ontario
M5A 1R7

Printed and bound in Canada

Contents

Editor's note

These stories are arranged according to reading level and narrative complexity, with the easier stories presented first.

The Troll

Jordan Wheeler

It lived in Colony Creek and had a voice like the *baa* of an angry sheep. It could be heard at night among the frogs' croaks and the sound of the crickets, warning the children to stay away.

To some it was a leprechaun, to others, a little person, but the children of Osborne Row knew it as the troll.

The legend said that long ago, a curse was laid, and an old man became trapped forever in a child's body. The body grew old, but stayed short. Some said the troll was smelly and ugly too. No one knew for sure.

The legend said the only way to break the curse was for the troll to pay a million cubits in gold walnuts and steal a child's thoughts. How much was a cubit? No one knew for sure.

The legend said the troll slept by day and worked by night, collecting walnuts along Colony Creek. He turned them to gold and hid them. No one ever found out where. No one ever found him. He couldn't be seen, but he could be heard among the frogs' croaks and the sound of the crickets, if you listened closely. With a voice like the *baa* of an angry sheep, or the snort of a sleeping bull, he warned you to stay away. But if the time was right, you would hear him say,

The moon is full,
It is a misty night,
I am the troll,
The time is right.

On a normal day, the children spent much of their time catching tadpoles in the creek or playing in the small forest beside it—running through the trails and climbing trees. Sometimes, they looked for the troll's treasure of golden walnuts, but they never found it.

So the children in the city of Osborne Row, in the suburb of Colony Heights, played at Colony Creek by day but stayed away at night. Especially when the moon was full on cool, misty nights.

"Is there really a troll in Colony Creek?" asked Jack Waboose.

"No one knows for sure," answered Billy Kwan.

Together, Jack Waboose and Billy Kwan sat on the west bank of Colony Creek watching others their age catching frogs. It was fall, and tadpoles only come out in the spring. By the time fall comes, they have grown into frogs.

"Do you believe it?"

"No, but just in case, I never come here at night."

"Me neither," said Jack Waboose, "just in case."

Nobody went down to Colony Creek at night. Not the children, not the milk-men, not the bus drivers, not the joggers, certainly not the lawyers, not even the policemen went down to Colony Creek at night. Of course, none of the adults believed in the troll, but still, at night, everyone stayed away. "Just in case," they would always say.

Jack Waboose and Billy Kwan didn't like frogs. They didn't even like tadpoles. While all the other boys their age would be jumping around the creek, Billy and Jack played either hackysack or Frisbee just beside the small forest. Since the forest was on the west side of the creek, and their homes were on the east side, every time they went they had to cross the bridge twice. It was an old bridge, a creepy bridge. If there really was a troll in Colony Creek, he surely lived under that bridge.

It was a warm day, considering it was fall in Osborne Row, the perfect day to throw the Frisbee. Jack liked Frisbee more than Billy. It was Jack's Frisbee and it was more valuable to him than his bike, even more than the family car. Jack really and truly loved that Frisbee. The hackysack belonged to Billy.

It was a warm day. Frogs don't like warm days, so the other boys couldn't find any. That was why, after two frustrating hours, they walked over to Billy and Jack. A tall boy named Bob Lawson stood in front.

"Hey Jack," he said, "can we play Frisbee too?"

They all knew they had to ask Jack. They all knew it was Jack's Frisbee.

Jack thought about it for a long time. So did Billy. They didn't know if they should let the others play Frisbee with them or not. Bob Lawson and his friends hadn't been too friendly to Billy and Jack over the summer. They had teased Jack because he had long, black braided hair, and they teased Billy because his parents couldn't speak English too well. In the end, Jack decided it was only fair. There were no frogs around and the others had nothing to do. He let them play Frisbee.

They played long and they played hard, throwing the white Frisbee high in the air. It was just before supper when it happened. Someone threw it too hard and it landed in the forest. For half an hour, everyone searched for Jack Waboose's Frisbee, but when suppertime came, everyone went home, except Billy and Jack.

"What are we going to do?" asked Jack.

"I don't know about you, but I'm going home for supper. I'm hungry."

Jack was hungry too.

"We could come back after supper. The two of us should be able to find it."

"Okay," said Billy, seeing as they were good friends, "but only for a little while." He didn't want to be there after dark, just in case.

"Okay," said Jack. Neither did he.

Supper came and went and Billy and Jack went back to Colony Creek alone. They started searching again through the forest. An hour went by, and the sun got lower, and another hour went by, and the sun was almost gone. While Billy and Jack searched, the rhyme kept going through their mind.

The moon is full,
It is a misty night,
I am the troll,
The time is right.

They both looked at the moon.

It wasn't full. There was no mist either. But still, it was getting dark, and Billy wanted to go home, just in case.

When he said this, Jack Waboose thought for a long time.

"No," he said at last. "I'm gonna stay and find my Frisbee after dark." He really loved that Frisbee.

"How are you gonna find it in the dark?"

"It glows in the dark."

"Jack."

"What?"

"You're nuts."

"I really love that Frisbee, Billy. Besides, there probably is no troll."

"You're probably right," Billy said uncertainly.

And so it got dark, and still they searched, but they could not find Jack's

Frisbee. After another two hours, they decided they had better go home.

"We'll look for it again tomorrow," said Jack, "after school."

"Okay," said Billy. "Let's go home."

Both boys turned and looked at the bridge, the old, creepy, wooden bridge. If there really was a troll in Colony Creek, it would surely live under that bridge, and Billy and Jack had to cross it. They walked towards it, trying not to listen to the crickets and the frogs.

"Where were you earlier?" Billy thought, referring to the frogs. They reached the bridge and started to cross it. Their footsteps echoed loudly. Half way across, Jack stopped.

"What's the matter?" asked Billy.

"I heard something," said Jack.

"No you didn't," Billy said, walking faster. When he reached the other side he stopped. Jack hadn't followed.

"Listen," said Jack.

And they listened, and in between the frogs' croaks and the sound of the crickets, they heard it. It sounded like an angry sheep or a sleeping bull and it said,

The moon is full,
It is a misty night.
I am the troll,
The time is right.

"Run!" yelled Billy.

And the boys ran faster than they ever had before. Up the hill on the east side, across Colony Street, and down Cricket Drive they ran. They ran until they could run no more, and so they stopped, huffing and panting.

"What was that?" gasped Billy.

"I'm not sure," said Jack.

They talked and thought, and thought and talked. What they had heard must be the troll, they both agreed for it came from Colony Creek, and it sounded like the *baa* of an angry sheep, or the snort of a sleeping bull.

"I don't understand though," said Jack. "He said the words, but there isn't any mist tonight, and the moon is not full."

"Maybe he made a mistake," said Billy.

"Do you want to go back and find out?"

"No way."

"Why not?"

"I don't want any troll stealing my thoughts."

"He can't, not tonight. There is no mist, and the moon is not full."

"I don't care," said Billy. "I'm not going back tonight."

"Okay," said Jack. "Then how about tomorrow?"

"No way," said Billy.

It was late and Billy and Jack walked home. All the way Billy kept repeating, "No way." They went to sleep in their own homes, and the troll filled their dreams. When morning came and Billy awoke, he said "No way." They went to school and into class, and Billy kept saying "No way." After supper, they started to play. Then Jack asked Billy if he would help look for the Frisbee. Billy thought for a long time, but finally said, "Okay."

So again they walked to Colony Creek and crossed the creepy bridge.

"This time," said Billy, "we're going home before it gets dark."

"Sure," said Jack, and they searched the forest for the Frisbee.

It was a warm day, but it was getting cool fast. They had searched for an hour when Billy stopped, needing a rest. He walked down to the creek and sat on the bank, staring into the cool, murky water. His feet were hot, so he took off his runners and socks and dipped his feet into the creek. The water felt pretty good, and he pressed his toes into the mud, wiggling them about. He felt a stone get stuck in between two of his toes. He pulled his foot out and grabbed the stone, ready to throw it away, but something caught his eye. He took a closer look.

Jack was still searching in the forest when he heard Billy yell for him.

"Jack! Come here, quick."

At first, Jack thought Billy had found his Frisbee, though it was strange that it was by the creek. He was sure he had seen it fly into the forest. When he got to the creek, he saw Billy standing in bare feet, holding up a golden walnut.

Darkness came, and Billy and Jack sat on the bridge. Jack was holding the golden walnut. It was a cloudy, cool night, and both boys became quite nervous when mist began to rise from Colony Creek.

"I'm scared," said Billy.

"Me too," said Jack, "But I'm also excited. He's here, I can feel it."

The frogs croaked and the crickets creaked, and then they heard the *baa* of an angry sheep, or was it the snort of a sleeping bull?

"Actually," said Jack, "it sounds a bit like my father when he snores."

Then came the words.

The moon is full,
It is a misty night,
I am the troll,
The time is right.

"Wait!" cried Jack. "It may be misty, but the moon is not full."

"Who's that?" growled the troll.

"Jack Waboose, and this is Billy Kwan."

"Hi," squeaked Billy.

"Ah, two young boys. You are brave, but you are wrong. Look above you."

Jack and Billy looked above. The clouds parted revealing a full moon.

"It is a full moon, is it not?" asked the troll.

"It looks that way," Jack gulped. Billy was getting ready to run away. "But is the time right?" Jack asked.

"I have a million cubits in golden walnuts, the time is right," said the troll. "Last night, I finally finished. Yes, the time is right. I am so glad you are here."

"He's gonna steal our thoughts," yelled Billy.

"You are right," growled the troll. "But do not run. I am too fast, you are too close, I will surely catch you. Just give up, like good little boys, and allow me your thoughts."

"I don't think the time is right," said Jack.

"What do you mean?" asked the troll.

"I believe you are one walnut short."

"Impossible!" growled the troll.

"You'd better check."

The troll was silent as he thought. Then he jumped out of the water and on to the bridge. He was short, and ugly, and he smelled bad. Billy pinched his nose. With mean, beady little eyes, the troll stared at Jack.

"How do you know I am missing one walnut?"

"Just a hunch," said Jack.

"Humph!" the troll growled. "Very well. I'll go and recount, but you have to stay here. Don't move or you'll be sorry."

Billy and Jack looked at each other.

"Okay," said Jack, "we'll stay here."

The troll, with his short clumsy little legs, walked past the boys and up the bank of the creek. He disappeared into the darkness.

"Now's our chance," said Billy. "Let's split."

"No," said Jack. "He's one walnut short. The time isn't right."

"What if he gets another one?"

"Good point," said Jack. "We'll wait by the road."

The boys left the bridge and walked back to the road. Several minutes later, the troll returned.

"Curses, curses, curses. You were right, I am one walnut short. The time is not right," said the troll. "Wait a minute. Where are you?"

"Over here," called Jack.

"You were supposed to wait down here, you little liars."

"We didn't trust you."

"Ah, what does it matter? I'm one walnut short, the time is not right. The hour of midnight approaches."

"What do you mean?" asked Jack.

"Tonight is the night. My only chance to break the evil curse. If I do not do it tonight, I will be stuck here forever."

"But if you break the curse, a child will lose his thoughts," said Billy.

"Only for a while," said the troll. "I am not evil. After I have finished, I will give them back. But alas, what does it matter now? I am one walnut short."

"Can't you find another one?" asked Jack.

"The walnut I lost was the last walnut in Colony Creek. There are none left."

The troll sat on the bridge, hanging his head low. All that work for so many years, for nothing. He was trapped forever.

"Have you seen a Frisbee?" asked Jack.

"A what?" asked the troll, sadly.

"A Frisbee. A round thing that flies through the air."

"Is it a golden Frisbee, a silver Frisbee, or a Frisbee lined with emeralds?" asked the troll.

"It is none of those," said Jack. "It is white and plastic."

"Yes, I have seen your Frisbee."

"Where?"

"I have it. I found it last night. It is a marvelous toy. I am going to take it." He sighed.

"It's my Frisbee." said Jack

"Oh," said the troll, "I suppose you want it back?"

"Yes."

"Well, you can buy another one."

"How about a trade?" said Jack.

"A trade? A trade for what?"

"You give me my Frisbee, and I'll give you a golden walnut."

"What's this? You have a golden walnut? Where did you get it?"

"I found it today. It's a marvelous toy. I was going to keep it," said Jack.

"Curses, you little thief. Give it back."

"First, give me my Frisbee."

"Oh, you're a sly young boy. But I don't have the Frisbee with me. It's in my home. I'll tell you what though. You give me the walnut, and I'll tell you how to get there."

"I don't trust you," said Jack.

"Come down here, where we can talk."

"Don't go," whispered Billy. "It's a trick."

"He's just a little guy," said Jack. "He can't hurt me."

In the misty moonlight Jack walked to the bridge. He could smell the troll.

"You smell bad," he said, as they came face to face.

"You would too," said the troll, "if you lived by a smelly creek all your life."

"If you do break the curse, where would you go?"

"Home, of course."

"Where's that?"

"I'd rejoin the little people in the Gardens of the Hesperides, where the apple trees bear golden fruit."

"Is that how you can turn walnuts into gold?"

"Yes, I can turn almost anything into gold."

"How about crab apples?"

"Crab apples? What are they?"

"Little apples that grow in trees. There is one in the Harrisons' back yard."

"I most certainly could turn crab apples into gold. Now give me my walnut."

Jack pulled the golden walnut out of his pocket and held it in his hand.

"What will happen if I give this to you?"

"Then I will borrow your thoughts."

"I still don't trust you."

The troll leapt at Jack, grabbing for the walnut. Jack pulled his hand away and the clumsy troll landed on his belly and bounced into the creek. He crawled out onto the bridge, wet and smelly.

"I won't hurt you, I promise," said the troll, lying down and pounding his fists on the wooden bridge like a child having a tantrum. "I just want to go home."

Something told Jack that the troll was telling the truth, but he was still worried about losing his thoughts, even for a little while.

"When you have a child's thoughts, what happens to the child?" he asked.

The troll stopped his crying and looked up.

"The child will have my thoughts."

"Is that how I will know where you live so I can get my Frisbee back?"

"That and a whole lot more," said the troll. "A new world will open up to you. You will see my home, my people, all of my thoughts, as I will see yours."

"Okay," said Jack, "I can dig that." He tossed the walnut into the troll's dirty little hands. The troll stood up and placed his hands on Jack's head.

Billy Kwan was still by the road, and he could barely see Jack and the troll through the mist. Then the mist cleared with a whoosh, and light glowed from the bridge. The glow surrounded Jack and the troll as they touched each other's heads. Then they began to rise. They floated up and over the creek, still glowing. Billy Kwan could hardly believe his eyes. Suddenly, the glowing stopped, and there was darkness once again. There was a splash as Jack fell into the creek. Billy ran down to see him.

"Where's the troll?" he asked.

"He's gone," said Jack, "to the Gardens of the Hesperides where the apple trees bear golden fruit."

"Where?"

"It's a beautiful place, Billy. I've seen it."

"What happened?"

"I gave the troll my thoughts, and he gave me his," said Jack, climbing out of the creek. "Come on."

"Where?"

"To get my Frisbee."

They walked along the bank until they came to a large tree hanging over the creek. They had seen the tree many times before. They had even climbed it, but it looked different as Jack crawled around the trunk close to the water's edge. Billy followed and found himself entering a small hole that led into a cave. Inside, they could stand up. It was a long cave and they had walked several metres when they came to a bed and dresser, and other things found in a normal house. There was even a small television.

"Wow!" was all that Billy could say.

They both turned to the bed. A disk lay on it; a bright, shiny glittering disk that spread light throughout the cave. Jack picked it up. It was his Frisbee. The troll had turned it to gold.

"Come on. Let's go," said Jack.

Some said it was a leprechaun, to others it was a little person, but the children of Osborne Row knew it as the troll, and it isn't there any more.

The Ebony Forest

Jordan Wheeler

"So how do you like it here so far?" Monica asked, her feet dangling in the water of Lake Manigatogan.

"So far, it's been okay," answered Milton.

"Okay? Is that it?"

"All right, it's been great, but I miss the video games at the seven-eleven."

"We have video games in town."

"I know, but they're old. I do like it here though. Especially the lake."

Milton was ten, and it was the first time he had ever been away from the city. His mother had sent him to stay with his uncle, Jake Whitehawk, for the summer. Monica was Jake's daughter,

Milton's cousin. So far he had been spending most of his time with her.

"It's getting late," said Monica. "We should leave soon."

"Do we have to?" asked Milton. "It's such a long walk."

"That's why we have to. Come on," she said, getting up.

"Okay," sighed Milton. "But why can't we walk through the forest? It would take half the time."

"The forest is a forbidden place. No one can walk through it."

Ebony Forest was small but dark, with tall dark trees and dense bush, and it stood between Lake Manigatogan and Caribou, the town where Monica and her father lived. For generations, the people of Caribou on the Wapaskwa Reserve had fished on Lake Manigatogan and had walked through the Ebony Forest every day. But something tragic had happened there several years ago and now, everyone walked around. Monica and Milton were now following that same path.

The sun was going down as they walked along the edge of the forest. The trees towered above them, blocking out the setting sun. Milton could hear squirrels chattering and crows cawing, sounds not heard in the city. He wanted to walk into the forest but knew he couldn't. No one could. He wondered what exactly had happened there. So far, no one had told him. Not even Monica.

Monica was walking ahead, leading the way, when Milton stopped.

"I have to go to the bathroom," he said.

"Hurry up," she told him. "Go behind one of the trees."

This was one of the things he liked about the country so far. You could go to the bathroom outside. He stepped into the forest, and heard a cry. He listened and it came again.

"Help me. Please."

Milton turned and listened. It sounded like it was coming from a young girl, and she was very close.

"Monica," he yelled, "someone is in there."

"In where?"

"The forest. It's a girl. She's calling for help."

"Knock it off Milton. Are you finished?"

"I'm serious. Come on, let's find her."

"Milton, come on. No one is in there. Hurry up, it's late."

He listened again. This time, he heard nothing.

"Hurry, it's getting dark," Monica said.

Milton hesitated, then walked out of the forest and followed his cousin to Caribou, but he was certain he had heard a young girl cry for help.

"You were probably hearing things," Monica told him, as they walked up to her house. "Besides, no one goes into the forest any more."

"Why not?" Milton asked.

"They just don't."

They entered the house just in time for supper. All through the meal Milton thought about the girl's cry. The memory of it followed him through the night and he became convinced it wasn't just imagined. He had really heard a girl's cry. Something told him he should ask about the Ebony Forest.

The following morning Milton got up early and followed his uncle to the truck.

"Can I go fishing with you today?" he asked.

"I'm going to be gone all day, Milt. You'd be better off staying with Monica. You'd have more fun."

"But I wanted to talk to you."

"About what?" asked Uncle Jake.

"Ebony Forest."

"What about Ebony Forest?"

"How come no one is allowed to go in there?"

"Because many years ago something terrible happened."

"What?"

Jake Whitehawk looked at Milton carefully. "Do you really want to know?"

"Yes."

"Then I believe you will find out on your own. Have a good time today. I'll see you later."

Jake got into the truck and drove off, leaving Milton somewhat puzzled. "How will I find out if no one will tell me?" he thought.

He turned and looked across the road at the forest. Even in the morning light, a darkness hung among the tall trees, and he remembered the cry for help he had heard the day before. He walked across the road and up to the forest, staring into it, searching the trees for an answer. The wind was blowing, and it whistled through the forest, and again he heard a cry.

"Please, help me. Milton, please."

"Milton!"

Milton turned around. Monica was calling him from across the road.

"What are you doing?"

He ran up to her. "I heard it again, Monica," he said.

"Come off it, will you?" Then she noticed the look on his face — a frightened look.

"What's wrong?"

"She called my name," said Milton.

"Who?"

"The girl's voice I heard yesterday."

"I told you before, no one is in that forest. No one is allowed."

"I swear Monica, I heard her. She called my name."

"Sure, and moose have purple spots. What do you want to do today?"

It was obvious that Monica wasn't going to believe him so he dropped the subject.

"Let's go swimming again," he suggested.

"Okay, but let's have breakfast first. I'm hungry."

They had breakfast, and they went swimming, again walking around the forest. He didn't hear the voice this time but hoped he would on the way back. They swam for a few hours in the cool, blue lake, soaking up the sun and enjoying the fresh air. It was late afternoon when they decided it was time to go home. As they walked past the forest, Milton kept listening for the girl's voice, but all he could hear were squirrels, birds, the wind, and Monica talking about her baseball team. He knew he had to get in closer.

"I have to go to the bathroom," Milton told her.

"Geez, Milt. Why didn't you go when we were at the lake? They have bathrooms there you know."

"I didn't have to go then. I'll make it quick," he said, running into the forest.

"You shouldn't be peeing in the forest," she yelled.

"I'll be finished in a second."

Of course, Milton didn't really have to go to the bathroom, he just used it as an excuse to go into the forest. He was about ten metres in when he stopped to listen. He was still able to see Monica through the trees. Suddenly, he again heard the girl, but this time, it wasn't a cry for help.

"Hi, Milton. I knew you would come."

Milton turned, and standing a few feet in front of him was a girl of his own age, wearing a deerskin dress with her hair in two long braids.

"Who are you?" asked Milton.

"Tanis, don't you remember? I knew you would come back. I knew you wouldn't leave me."

"Hurry up!" yelled Monica.

"I have to go," said Milton.

"No, don't leave me again."

"I'll be back, I promise."

"You promise?"

"Yes."

"All right, but do something for me."

"What?"

"Say hi to my sister. I miss her so much. We were so close."

"Who's your sister?"

"Don't be silly. Jenny Whitehawk, who else."

"Milton," Monica called.

"Okay, I'll say hi to her. I have to go."

"Promise you will come back?"

"I promise."

Milton watched the girl disappear into the forest, then he rejoined Monica.

"What took so long?"

"I had to go bad."

"Oh."

While they walked back to Caribou, Monica did all the talking. Milton's thoughts were on the girl, Tanis. She was pretty, he thought. He wondered what she was doing out there, and why she thought she knew him.

That night at supper Milton asked Uncle Jake about Jenny Whitehawk.

"Do you know her?"

"Jenny Whitehawk, huh? Who is she?"

"My mom wanted me to say hi to her."

"The only Jenny Whitehawk I know is Jennifer Courchene. She's a widow, but her last name was Whitehawk before she got married."

"Do you know where I could find her?"

"Sure, she lives at the edge of town. It's an old, green house along the highway. I didn't know your mother knew her. She is a distant relative though."

The next day, Milton went off to find Jennifer Courchene's house on the edge of town. Caribou isn't a large town so it wasn't a long walk. He found her house without much trouble. He walked up and knocked on the door. An old woman answered.

"Hello," she said.

"Jennifer Courchene?" Milton asked.

"Yes."

"And Jenny Whitehawk?"

A strange look came over the old woman's face, then she smiled.

"I haven't heard that name in a long time. Where did you hear it?"

"I'm Jake Whitehawk's nephew, Dolores Whitehawk's son. I think we're related to you somehow."

"Everyone on this reserve is related to each other somehow. Come on in. You want some tea?"

Milton had never had tea before. His mom wouldn't let him, but he thought he might like to try it.

"Sure," he said, "I'll have a cup."

Jennifer poured two cups of tea and they sat at the kitchen table. She stared at him for several moments.

"You look terribly familiar," she said at last.

"My name is Milton Whitehawk."

Another strange look came over the woman's face.

"Did you say Milton Whitehawk?"

"Yes."

"That's another name I haven't heard in quite some time. Come to think of it, that's who you remind me of."

"Who?" Milton asked, taking his first sip of tea.

"Milton Whitehawk."

"Who's he?" Milton asked, taking his second sip of tea.

"He was my brother. This is odd. You come here bearing my name that hasn't been used in fifty years and you are the spitting image of my dead brother who had the same name you have. Tell me, what brought you here?"

"I was told to say hi to a Jenny Whitehawk, and you are the only Jenny Whitehawk I could find," Milton said, deciding he didn't like tea.

"Who sent you?"

"A girl named Tanis."

"Oh!" the woman cried. She covered her face with her hands as tears came to her eyes. "Why are you saying these things? Why are you bringing back forgotten names, and forgotten memories?"

"But I saw her."

"Where?"

"In the Ebony Forest. First she cried for help, then she cried for help and called my name. Then the third time I heard her was when I saw her. She seemed to know me and said she knew I would come back. She was wearing a deerskin dress and had her hair in two long braids. She was really pretty. I told her I had to go, but she made me promise to say hi to her sister, Jenny Whitehawk. That's why I came here. She says she really misses you. You do look a little old to be her sister though."

Now the woman had another strange look on her face, stranger than before. Her eyes were wide and she was staring at Milton with horror. She grabbed his head and looked behind his left ear.

"You have a birthmark?"

"I've had it all my life."

The woman let go. Milton grabbed his ear.

"My mom said it looks like a seven. Is Tanis really your sister?"

"Yes," said the old woman, with shiny eyes. "Please leave me alone now. I have to decide what to do."

Milton did as the old woman asked. He walked back to his uncle's house and sat on the front steps, not really sure if the old woman believed him. About half an hour later, she came walking up to him.

"Do you believe me?" Milton asked.

"I believe you. Now take me to Tanis," said Jennifer Whitehawk, still looking somewhat strange.

They walked across the road and into the Ebony Forest with Milton leading the way. They walked a great distance into the forest before stopping.

"I'm back," said Milton.

"I knew you would come back," came the voice.

"Tanis?" whispered Jennifer.

From behind a tree came the girl in the deerskin dress.

"Jenny, my sister. It's so good to see you again."

"Oh Tanis."

"Milton came back. I knew he would. Our brother isn't evil after all. Now we are reunited, and now I may rest."

"I did not think I would live to see this day," said Jennifer. "I didn't believe it. Not until I saw the birthmark."

"The seven behind his ear," said Tanis. "You have done your part Milton, you came back. Now please leave us. I want to learn all about my sister's life before I rest. Perhaps Jenny may choose to come and rest with me."

Tanis walked up to Milton and hugged him. "I had faith in you, my brother. Now go."

Milton did as she wished. He left them alone and walked out of the Ebony Forest. His uncle was sitting on the steps when he reached the house. Milton sat beside him.

"So did you learn about the Ebony Forest?" asked Jake.

"I'm not sure," Milton said. "Could you please tell me?"

"A long time ago," his uncle began, "there was a young boy and a young girl who wandered into the Ebony Forest. They were brother and sister. The story is that they found something very valuable and were going to take it back to town, but the young boy got greedy, wanting what they had found for himself. He pretended that they were lost and left his sister in the forest. Only he couldn't find his way out either. They found his body three days later, but they never found the girl's. People say that her spirit wandered the forest calling out his name for several years until it stopped about ten years ago. That is why no one is allowed to go into the Ebony Forest."

"The girl's name was Tanis and the brother's name was Milton Whitehawk, just like mine," said Milton, "and I was born ten years ago."

"How did you know?"

"Because Tanis called me."

"So Tanis's spirit called out to you. I guess she must have thought you were her brother returning to find her after all these years. Why did you ask about Jenny Whitehawk though?"

"Tanis wanted to see her sister."

"Did you see Tanis?"

"Yeah, she was real pretty. I didn't know she was a ghost though."

"It's good you did what you did. Tanis was waiting for her brother to return and find her, and after she died, her spirit kept waiting. Now that you found her, her waiting is over. Her spirit can finally rest."

"I think maybe Jenny will rest with her."

"That would be nice. They used to be really close."

"Just think, none of this would have happened unless I came out here to spend the summer."

"I don't know," said Uncle Jake. "Tanis would have reached you somehow."

"Did they ever find the thing of value that Tanis and Milton found?"

"No. Milton must have dropped it somewhere before he died. No one ever found anything."

"What was it?"

"No one knows for sure, but the stories say it might have been a squirrel's nest full of golden walnuts."

"Well," Milton said. "Now I know why the Ebony Forest is a forbidden place."

"It's over now," Uncle Jake told him. "It doesn't have to stay forbidden."

Milton thought for a moment. He thought about Tanis, and Jenny, and a boy named Milton. "It should stay forbidden," he said finally. "It's their private place."

"Hey, Milton. Want to go swimming?" It was Monica, standing by the door in her bathing suit.

Milton smiled. "Sure," he said.

Adventure on Thunder Island

Edna King

Jessica clutched the wildflowers she had picked for her grandmother. A wasp tried to land on her bouquet but she swatted it away with her free hand. It flew back at her and buzzed around her face. She swatted it a second time, then ran as fast as she could down the gravel road.

Out of breath, she stopped at a rocky hill and spread her collection on a rock, fingering each one delicately. She knew Nokomis, her grandmother, would be pleased. Sighing, she sat beside them on the rock and gazed breathlessly at the sky, watching the fluffy grey clouds take animated shapes as they floated by.

She smiled at one cloud shaped like a headband filled with feathers hovering over Thunder Island. If a headdress belonged anywhere, it would certainly be there. After all, Thunder Island was the burial place of tribal chiefs and medicine people. She had been told that their spirits waited for the people who chose to carry on traditions.

In the distance she could see dark clouds nearing her community, the First Nations of Eagle's Nest, home of the Ojibwa. The dampness in the air and the cool breeze blowing through the trees told her that it would rain soon, and rain hard. She quickly stood up and started down the road towards home.

The little road twisted and turned along the lake. She skipped along, humming softly. Then she stopped. Ahead of her, on the other side of thick shrubs, she could hear voices. Creeping forward, she peeked between the branches and saw her brother Philip and his best friend

Nathan rowing their homemade raft ashore. Smiling to herself, she crouched down, then suddenly leapt out from behind the bush toward them. "Rah!" she shouted.

Both boys jumped, nearly sinking their raft. "Jessie!" roared Philip in anger.

She laughed, "Hah! I did it! I really scared you that time."

Philip jumped ashore. "I think I hear Dad calling you." He helped Nathan ashore and they tried to pull in the raft together.

"Oh," she sulked, "don't take it out yet. Can't I go for a ride?"

"Not today," Philip huffed as he and Nathan struggled with the heavy raft.

"But you told me this morning I could," she persisted.

Philip fell on his behind as the raft stubbornly landed. "Not today, Jess! Okay?" Then he saw the hurt look in his little sister's face. "Tomorrow, Nathan and I will row you all around the lake."

She smiled, "Okay, just remember—tomorrow for sure." Turning, she walked to the road and continued on her way.

When she reached the house she found her father by the pick-up truck. The hood of the truck was open and he was looking inside. "Oh, kwe-sainse, how are you on this fine afternoon?" he said, looking up.

"I'm fine," she smiled. Then she looked inside the engine. "What are you doing, Daddy?"

"Fixing her up," he said as he began banging something with a wrench. "Have you seen your brother?"

"He's down by the rocks with Nate."

"They're not on that old raft again, are they?"

"Yup."

"He was supposed to be back fifteen minutes ago. We have to go into town to pick up some supplies for Noko."

"I'll go and get him, Daddy," she volunteered.

She watched him get in behind the wheel of the truck. He started it up. It revved and kept going. "You did it, Daddy!" she exclaimed. He flashed her a smile as he got out of the cab and bent over the engine again. Not really wanting to disturb him, she asked anyway, "Daddy can I go with you, too?"

"Kwe-sainse, I think it would be better if you helped Noko. Can you do that for me, Jessica? Please?"

"Okay," she sighed. Remembering the flowers, she handed them to him saying, "Can you give these to Noko for me while I'm gone?" Not waiting for an answer, she turned and ran down the road to where she had last seen her brother.

When she got back to the raft, Philip and Nathan had left. She heard shouting deep in the woods and recognized her brother's voice. Jessica was getting ready to follow the voices when a wave crept ashore, soaking her foot. She noticed that waves were splashing the raft, causing it to move a little. She watched as another wave slapped against the raft, inching it a little more into the lake.

Jessica looked at the sky. When it started to rain, it would probably rain for a long time, maybe even all day tomorrow and maybe even the next day too. By that time, Philip would have forgotten all about the ride he had promised her.

Philip and Nathan's voices were moving farther away. She was sure that he was going home. She looked at the raft. It looked heavy. At the same time that Jessica pushed it, a wave splashed ashore, easily setting the raft afloat. She jumped on board and clutched the steering pole in her hands.

Singing to herself, she let the waves carry the raft. The cold wind was making her long hair fly about, and she tried to keep one of her hands free to brush it off her face. Thinking she was far enough out, she decided it was time to head home. With the steering pole, she tried to push the raft towards shore.

It was very hard for the little girl to steer. The pole was too long and the waves were high. Struggling, she tried to push the raft but the ferocious waters fought back. It seemed as though an invisible hand underneath the waters held it tight. She tried hard to move it. It jerked loose, while at the same time the pole snapped in half. Jessica was tossed roughly to the floor but held on to keep herself from going overboard.

Jessica cried softly. She wondered why she hadn't admitted to herself just how choppy the waves had become. She felt so small as tall waves blanketed her, but still she held tight. The raft beating against the waves filled her ears with the same rhythm as pow-wow drums. With each beat she could hear, "Hold tight. Stay calm."

She looked toward shore. It seemed very far away. For an instant she thought she saw her father and Philip, but she couldn't be sure. The thought of never seeing them again made her cry even more.

Jessica held tightly to the raft while thick, dark storm clouds surrounded her. Thunder was rumbling now, and she didn't want to even think about the lightning that went along with it. The rain had just started, but she didn't care because she was already soaked. She hadn't noticed that she was drifting towards Thunder Island.

No one from Eagle's Nest could remember when Thunder Island was named. They only knew it was an island that had once been used for sacred ceremonies. Jessica's father once told her that young men, and sometimes women, used to go there to seek visions that would guide them through life. The Ojibwa of Eagle's Nest still considered it sacred.

Jessica could no longer see the mainland. A change in the rhythm of the wind told her that she was near land and that land could only be Thunder Island.

Her feet touched the soft, wet sand and she turned with a frantic jerk and crawled up the beach. She wanted to laugh because she had beaten the stormy waters, but instead, she sat on the ground and sobbed. A loud crash of thunder startled her, scaring away any other shocks from her boat ride. She tried to make her tired body stand. Slowly she walked up the shore, hoping to find shelter somewhere on the island.

Lightning flashed, brightening the blackened sky. She could hear the wind blowing through the trees. It sent shivers up and down her spine. She was cold and could feel her body tremble all over. Her Nokomis had always told her to wear a sweater. She wished she had a sweater now. She wished she had her grandmother now. She longed so much for the comforting hug her grandmother would give her. Nokomis always knew when she needed to be held and she needed her Noko now like never before. Oh, poor, poor Noko, she must be so worried! And Jessica was so hungry. She was supposed to help her Noko with supper. Cold. Hungry. Tired. Jessica didn't think she could ever be all three at once.

Jessica found a tall pine and sat under it in a bed of fallen pine needles. She knew that she must be missed by now, but would they find out that she had taken the raft? And even if they did, how would they know where the raft had gone? How could they even begin to search for her on the lake, especially in this storm?

The wind and the rain, together with the thunder, sang through the air in mock chorus. The lightning was flashing from different directions revealing weird shapes.

She could hear her name being whispered ever so softly. Once when she looked up she thought she saw her mother standing near her, beside a pine, but she knew that it could not be true because her mother had died just that winter. She closed her eyes to block out visions that tried to crawl inside her head.

Just when she felt brave enough to open her eyes, she watched as the lightning struck a tree branch close by. As she heard the crack of the branch, she closed her eyes to wait for the sound of the thunder that would follow.

As the thunder roared, Jessica felt something touch her cheek. She whimpered and brushed her face with her hand. Keeping her eyes closed, she hugged herself tightly. The she felt a warm hand on her forehead. Quickly, she shook her head to force it away. "No," she whispered.

"It's all right," crooned a soft voice over her head.

She opened her eyes slowly and, there, standing in front of her, was a tall young man. She was frightened and tried to push herself away from him, but the tree she leaned against held her in place.

"Don't be afraid," he said, smiling down at her. The smile lit up his whole face. His deep, dark eyes danced with the flashing light. His high cheek bones glowed, and his black shoulder-length hair blew freely in the wind. Jessica stared in disbelief.

"You're cold," he said softly. "Come with me, my child."

She looked into his face and blinked. He had a gentle face, a peaceful face. She reached for his hand and he lifted her.

His movements were swift and light. He never stumbled over any branches, protruding tree roots or holes in the ground. The thunder and lightning never startled him.

It didn't seem long before they reached a cave on a rocky hill. Once inside, he put her down. There was a fire flickering on the floor, not far from the mouth of the cave.

"Sit close to the fire," he told her.

She did, in a place were she could watch every move he made. He brought a large pot to the fire. "You must be hungry," he said. He gave her a piece of frybread. She bit into it. It was good. Just as good as the ones Nokomis made.

She watched him walk to the back and return with a blanket. He put it over her shoulders and wrapped it around her. "This will keep you warm." The blanket smelled of moosehide and it was soft like rabbit's fur. Jessica snuggled tightly inside and watched him kneel in front of the fire. He put some stew in a bowl, then handed it to her. Ooh, it smelled so good! "Take this," he said softly. "It will warm you inside."

"Thank you," she said.

She nibbled her fry-bread in between sips of stew. He wasn't eating with her, but he too sat near the fire. He had a small piece of wood in his hand. He reached inside a small pocket on his waistband and pulled out a little knife. He turned to her and met her glance. He smiled, "Are you warming up yet?"

She nodded.

Then he began to carve vigorously. As she ate, she studied him. He was dressed differently from her daddy or her uncle David. He was dressed almost like he was going to a pow wow, but without all the beads, bone necklaces, and feathers. Everything he wore looked as if it was made of hide.

She finished her meal and put down her wooden bowl and examined it carefully. He must have made it, too!

"Would you like some more, Jessica?" he asked. "There is plenty to eat."

"No thanks," she replied, watching him closely. "How do you know my name?"

He laughed loudly and heartily. "I know the names of all my children."

She blinked. "Who are you, anyway?"

He set down everything he had in his hands and smiled at her. "I am Thunderchild, son of Thunder and son of Moon. I am son of Generations Past and Generations Not Yet Born."

Moon? Thunder? Maybe that's what his mom and dad called each other, the way her parents called each other "dear" and "honey."

He interrupted her thoughts. "It is time for you to sleep. Your father will be here to pick you up in the morning."

She argued, "No. I don't think so. He's not going to know where to find me."

"He will know," laughed Thunderchild. "Lie down, my child. Sleep."

He watched as she made herself comfortable on the ground and then covered herself with the blanket. He continued with his carving.

"What are you making, Mr. Thunder-child?" she asked.

"A totem," he answered.

"Oh," she said. "Mr. Thunderchild, do you know my daddy?"

"Yes," he answered, "I know your daddy. I spoke to him when he was young. I also know he will be here for you in the morning, so you should try to sleep."

She stifled a yawn. "But I'm not tired," she insisted. She began to wonder about Mr. Thunderchild and all the things he said he knew. How did he come to know these things? Where were his mom and dad now, and exactly how many children did he really have? But before she got the chance to ask him, she closed her eyes and fell asleep.

She awakened the next morning in a dark cave. The fire had burnt out. The only light she could see were rays of sunlight peeking through the cave door.

"Mr. Thunderchild!" she shouted. She could see that he was not around.

She walked outside and tried to blink away the sunlight that greeted her warmly. The air smelled fresh and clean. Leaves glistened with droplets from the night's rainfall. Her feet sank into the wet ground.

Jessica looked around for any sign of her new friend. "Mr. Thunderchild," she shouted again. Maybe he was down by the lake. She ran down a path calling his name. "Thunderchild! Where are you?!"

She reached the water's edge and looked up and down the rugged shore. He was nowhere to be seen. Then she heard a motor running. She looked out over the lake and saw her father coming towards the island in her uncle's boat. "Daddy!" she shouted.

She ran to greet him when he landed and he scooped her up and hugged her. "Kwe-sainse, I was so worried. Everyone was." Then he took her shoulders firmly between his hands, looked into her face and sternly said, "Don't ever do this again." Then he hugged her all over.

She squirmed out of his grip and said, "Come on, Daddy. You've got to help! We've got to find Thunderchild!"

"What are you talking about, Jessica?" he asked. "Who do we have to find?"

"Thunderchild, Daddy," she burst out. "You'll like him! Come on, let's find him!" She took his hand and pulled him in the direction of the cave. "He lives over this way."

As they walked, she told him all about the fire, the stew and the fry-bread. Her father listened, trying to make sense of it all.

When they neared the cave, she ran ahead. "Come on, Daddy, over here," and she quickly disappeared inside.

Inside the cave, they looked around. It was deserted. It didn't look as if there had been a fire burning. There were no ashes. There was no pot of stew. He looked at Jessica in silence.

She was disappointed. "This is the wrong cave, Daddy. It must be. Come on. Let's go find the right one."

They looked around again. The rocks were covered with dust and moss. He kicked at a worn piece of hide. It was chewed and thin. Could his daughter have stayed in this place?

"Daddy," her voice begged. "Come on. We've got to find Thunderchild!"

She was tugging his arm anxiously when he nearly tripped over something wrapped around his foot. He bent down to pick up a leather string. On the string hung a small carving.

Jessica took a close look at what he found. "That's what Mr. Thunderchild was making," she gasped. "But this can't be the place I stayed. This can't be..."

Suddenly, her father cut her off. "It's okay, kwe-sainse."

"But Daddy..."

He understood now, and placed the tiny carving in her hand. She felt the crevices, the pointed tips, the smoothness. She ran it lightly along her cheek. "It's his," she whispered.

"Here," her father said, "let me put it on you."

"No," she protested. "This is his. We should find him and give it to him."

"Kwe-sainse," her father tried to explain, "he made it for you. It's a gift."

"But..."

"He doesn't want you to look for him yet. He wants you to come and find him later...when you're older...after you've learned more about him and his family."

Jessica looked at her father. He was talking strangely, sounding like Thunderchild. Why couldn't grown-ups get to the point? "What do you mean?" she asked.

"Thunderchild has some secrets to tell you. Some day, you'll have to come to listen. And," he smiled at his daughter, "I think he'd appreciate it if you wore this," he added, pointing to the bird.

Very softly she explained, "He called it a totem."

"It is a totem. His legend name is Thunderbird. This carving also resembles the eagle. To you he is Hawk."

"Hawk," she repeated, holding her necklace close. It felt special.

"Can I put it on you now?" he asked.

She handed it to him then turned to let him fasten it. He smiled proudly, "We'd better go home to let Nokomis know you're all right."

As they left the cave, she stopped and glanced around once more. "Thank you, Thunderchild," she said to the still air. Then they left.

A lone figure emerged from a ledge at the top of the cave. He jumped to the ground and followed them.

Every now and then Jessica would turn around and look back down the path, but Thunderchild knew he couldn't be seen this time.

Invisible as a spirit sometimes is, he stood on a rock and watched them board the boat. The man and child looked back to shore but all they could see were rocks and trees cluttering the shoreline.

As the boat made a quick turn towards Eagle's Nest, a large bird flew up to a high tree. "See you later, Jessica," called the bird, flapping his huge dark wings.

She imagined that for a moment she heard his voice and turned to listen. All that she could feel was the wind blowing against her necklace.

Thunderchild smiled to himself, flew to the ground, and walked down the path towards the cave. He knew he'd see her again.

Pigeon Bridge

Jordan Wheeler

It was a hot day. Troy sat in the shade of his front yard staring up through the trees at the clear, blue sky, wondering what his new school would be like in the fall.

Summer had just begun and already Troy missed school. It wasn't having to sit in a classroom all day that he missed, or all the work he had to do. What he really missed were all his friends. Now that summer was here, he didn't see them. They had either gone out of town or now lived too far away. A week before, Troy and his family had moved into a new neighbourhood, far away from his old school, and far away from his friends.

Troy had seen lots of people close to his age on his new street, but he didn't know them. He was too shy to walk up and introduce himself. He watched as several boys came out of a house across the street, laughing and playing around. There were five of them and as they walked down the street, Troy wished he was part of the fun. As it was, he would probably spend another day by himself, or with his little sister, Missy. He heard the front door open behind him and he thought it was her.

"Troy, astum."

It was his kookum, or grandmother. He recognized her voice, and she was the only one in the family who still spoke Cree. He turned around and walked towards her.

"Kekwan?" he asked, showing her he still remembered some of the words she had taught him.

"Go to the store for me," she said, passing him a ten-dollar bill. "I need some flour."

"Can I buy something?"

"Okay, but nothing expensive, and bring back all the change."

The store was a few blocks away. Troy had been there a couple of times already. As he walked in, he noticed several people waiting in line ahead of him. He grabbed a bag of Robin Hood flour and took his place in line, thankful the store had air conditioning. The walk hadn't been far, but under the hot sun, beads of sweat had formed on his forehead.

When his turn came, Troy put the flour on the counter and asked for a slurp, just the thing for such a hot day. The cashier, a short man with glasses, put the flour in a bag, gave Troy his drink and the change and then turned to the next person in line, a girl about the same age as Troy. She too asked for a slurp.

"That will be fifty cents," said the cashier.

The girl put the money on the counter.

"You're ten cents short," he told her.

"That's funny. I'm sure I had enough when I came in."

Troy was still in the store. Overhearing them, he walked over and put a dime on the counter. The cashier smiled and handed a slurp to the girl.

"Thanks," she said, turning to Troy. Then she looked startled. "You're Indian," she said.

"Yeah, and you're white," said Troy.

He turned and walked out of the store. He was used to being treated differently because of his colour, but it still made him mad. The hot sun added to his discomfort.

The girl came running out of the store behind him.

"Hey, wait a minute," she yelled.

Troy stopped and turned around.

"I'm sorry I said that. I didn't mean anything by it," she said.

"Then why did you say it?"

"I don't know. It just popped out. I didn't expect you to be Indian."

"Us people are just like you people."

"I know. My name is Gina. What's yours?"

"Troy."

"Do you live around here?"

"Pretty close. I just moved here last week."

"That's why I haven't seen you before. You'll like it here. There's lots of neat things to do. Where do you live?"

"1250 Pigeon Street."

"Awesome! I live right across the street. Come on, I'll walk with you for a bit."

Gina showed Troy a short cut home through the back lanes, and told him who lived in all the houses they passed.

"See that big, blue house?"

"Which one?"

"With all the clothes out on the line. Billy Barton lives there. He hangs out with my brother."

Suddenly, a small object flew through the air and hit Gina in the stomach. "Ouch! Quick, over here."

She grabbed Troy's arm and ducked behind a fence as dozens of the small objects landed about them. "What are they?" Troy asked.

"Crab apples," said Gina. "Billy and Frank are in the Harrisons' yard again."

"Who's Frank?"

"My brother. They always climb into that tree when the Harrisons are out. It has the best crab apples in the neighbourhood, but Frank and Billy throw them at people instead of eating them. I think more of his friends are up there too."

"Hey Gina. Who's your new boyfriend?" someone yelled.

"Shut up, ape face," she shouted back.

Her reply caused another flurry of crab apples to come flying at them as Troy became quite embarrassed. He had never had a girlfriend before. "Don't let them bother you. They're idiots. Come on, we'll sneak through this yard."

Staying low, they crawled past the apple tree, hidden by a fence in the neighbouring yard. Troy could see the boys in the tree. It was the same group of five he had seen earlier. They made it safely past the tree and were walking between the houses when Gina finally stood up.

"You guys are idiots," she yelled. "We walked right by you." Another flurry of crab apples came their way. Gina again grabbed Troy as one of the small fruit hit him in the back.

"Quick, out the front."

"Ouch!"

When they reached the front yard, Gina suddenly stopped. "Uh oh." A large red car pulled up and stopped in front of them. "The Harrisons are home."

Four people got out of the car. "The kids are in our tree again," yelled a mean-looking man with a bushy beard and black curly hair. He was staring right at Troy.

"Quick, let's split," whispered Gina. The pair turned and ran with two of the Harrisons running after them.

"Here they come again," cried someone in the tree. Several crab apples hit

Gina and Troy as they ran. This time, they didn't hurt, but the Harrisons noticed.

"The Harrisons are home," someone in the tree shouted.

As Troy and Gina hit the back lane, five boys dropped out of the Harrisons' crab apple tree. Two were grabbed by the man. The other three made it to the lane and ran in the direction Troy and Gina took. They all stopped behind Gina and Frank's house, breathing hard from the run. Troy and Gina had dropped their slurps in the Harrisons' yard, but Troy was still carrying his kookum's bag of flour.

"Way to get us into trouble," said Frank, one of the three who had escaped.

"If it wasn't for us, you would still be up in the tree," said Gina. "None of you would have got away."

"Maybe. Who's your friend?"

"Troy," Gina introduced him. "And this is Billy Barton, Wally Wescott, and my brother, Frank."

"Hi," said Troy, looking at the three boys. Frank was the tallest, Billy Barton was the shortest, and Wally Wescott had blonde, curly hair that hung over his eyes. Every few seconds, Wally would shake his head so his hair would move away, but it always fell back.

"Hi," said Billy Barton and Wally Wescott.

"Gina, you know Dad doesn't want us to hang out with Indians," Frank told her.

"Shut up, Frank. He's my friend and I'll hang out with him if I want."

"Dad isn't going to like it."

"Dad doesn't have to know."

"He will if I tell him."

"You do that and I'll tell him about Pigeon Bridge."

"You wouldn't."

"I would."

Gina and Frank faced each other, daring one another to get them in trouble with their father. Billy Barton stuck his hands in his pockets, worried that if Frank's parents found out about Pigeon Bridge, all their parents would. Wally Wescott worried too, shaking his head nervously. Troy didn't know what

Pigeon Bridge was, and right now, he didn't care. He felt mad because of what Frank said, embarrassed because he was left out, but also glad that Gina stuck up for him.

"Come on, guys," Frank said, backing down. "Let's get out of here." Billy Barton and Wally Westcott turned and started walking away. Frank stayed behind to get in one last word. "Okay, hang out with him if you want, but don't expect me to."

"I wouldn't hang out with you anyway," said Troy, making a mean-looking face.

"Don't worry about it," said Frank, walking away.

Gina and Troy started walking away also, towards Troy's home. They were silent for a few seconds, but then Troy spoke. "Thanks."

"What for?"

"For sticking up for me."

"Don't worry about it."

"Okay, I won't, but thanks anyway."

"You're welcome."

"What's Pigeon Bridge?"

"It's a railroad bridge where my brother and his friends sometimes hang out. No trains go over it anymore because it's too old. Our parents don't let us go there, but Frank and them go anyway."

"Why is it called Pigeon Bridge?"

"Because it's at the end of Pigeon Street, and the bridge is full of pigeons."

"Birds?"

"Yup. Frank and his buddies always try to catch them. Sometimes they get lucky. Frank was the last one to catch one."

"What happens to the pigeons?"

"They sell them to the restaurants for a buck."

"Yuck."

"That's what I say. Uh oh."

"What?"

"My dad's home. I have to go."

"See ya."

"Bye."

Gina ran across the street and met her father, a big, heavy-set man with a thick, curly moustache. Troy wondered why he didn't like Indians. He wondered why anybody didn't like Indians. People were strange, but not Gina. He was glad she wasn't like her father or her brother. He went inside and gave his kookum her bag of flour and the change from the ten-dollar bill.

"What are you gonna do today?" asked his kookum.

"I don't know. Just hang out in the front yard, I guess."

"What do you mean hang out? From the window or off the roof?"

Troy laughed.

An hour later, Troy was sitting on his lawn. It was still hot. He was staring up at the sky again, resting after kicking his hackysack around. There was only one cloud he could see. A small, greyish ball of fluff, floating lazily across his line of sight. Oddly, it crossed paths with the sun, and suddenly the fluff was glowing. As shade covered Pigeon Street, two boys walked past Troy's yard holding their bellies. Troy thought he recognized them, and they recognized him.

"You're the guy Gina was with in the Harrisons' yard," said the short, pudgy one.

"We got caught," said the one with red hair and freckles.

"Sorry," said Troy. "Why are you holding your bellies?"

The two boys hesitated, then the short, pudgy one spoke. "When Mr. Harrison caught us, he made us eat fifty crab apples each."

"Oh," said Troy, trying hard not to laugh.

"Do you know where Frank and them went?" asked Tim Curly, the boy with red hair and freckles.

"I'm not sure. They said something about Pigeon Bridge."

Suddenly, the short, pudgy boy bent over in pain.

"What's wrong?" asked Tim.

"I have to go. It's an emergency."

The two boys looked around, then looked at Troy. "Can he borrow your bathroom?" Tim asked. The short, pudgy boy looked at Troy pleadingly.

"Okay," said Troy, "but only if you take me with you to Pigeon Bridge."

"No problem," said the boy, running into Troy's house. Troy followed him in.

"It's upstairs and to the right," he said.

Troy's kookum came out of the kitchen. "What's wrong with that boy?"

"He just ate fifty crab apples."

"Hah! Going to the bathroom, eh?"

Half an hour later, the short, pudgy boy, whose name was Trent Tarkenton, finally came out. Trent, Troy, and Tim started walking to Pigeon Bridge. Gina ran out of her house and caught up to them.

"Troy, where are you going?"

"They're taking me to Pigeon Bridge."

"What for?"

"I want to see it."

"It's dangerous, Troy."

"I just want to see it, Gina."

Gina thought for a moment. "Okay, but I'm coming with you."

It wasn't a long walk, but it was a hard one. They had to go through a large thicket of bushes that separated the bridge from a park at the end of Pigeon Street. There was nothing to suggest there was a bridge anywhere nearby, but when they came out, there it was. Troy could see that it was a very old bridge. The metal rails were full of rust and parts of the structure were falling apart. There was a sign warning people to stay away.

"I don't see them," said Trent Tarkenton.

"They're probably underneath," said Gina, walking onto the bridge. The boys followed.

As he walked out, Troy looked down between the railroad ties and could see a small creek running through the gorge the bridge spanned. It was a deep gorge and the creek was far below. The sound of pigeons cooing could be heard as they got further out. "How do you get underneath?" Troy wondered, still looking down.

"Just up ahead. You have to climb through a hole," Gina told him.

"What's underneath?"

"It's full of metal beams that support the bridge. They're pretty easy to climb around on, unless you're afraid of heights. There it is." Gina pointed to the hole. Tim Curly climbed through and disappeared from sight. Gina followed him. Trent Tarkenton sat down beside the hole, looking kind of nervous.

"Aren't you going down?" asked Troy.

"No way. I'm afraid of heights."

Troy poked his head into the hole and saw Gina standing on a metal beam just below.

"You coming?" she asked.

Troy pulled his head out, then lowered his feet and legs through, feeling for the beam. When he found it, he climbed through. He saw a maze of black metal beams running all through the underside of the bridge. It seemed almost impossible that anyone could ever fall. But if they did, they wouldn't live, he thought, looking down. There were pigeons all over the place, though not quite close enough to grab.

"Catching them should be easy," said Troy.

"Not that easy," said Gina, pointing to Frank and the others. They were further out and Troy watched as they grabbed for the birds. Each time someone came close, the birds would jump further away. When Tim Curly reached Frank, Billy, and Wally, they all stopped and turned to look at Troy and Gina.

"What did you bring him here for?" demanded Frank.

"'Cause he let Trent use his washroom," said Tim. "He had to go bad, Frank, and we were right in front of his house. He made us make a deal."

"You guys get out of here," Frank yelled at Troy and Gina. "This is our place."

"It's a free country, Frank. We can be here if we want," Gina replied.

There were a few moments of silence as Frank thought. "All right," he finally said. "If your friend here is brave enough to crawl down, maybe he could come over and help us catch some pigeons. That is if he isn't too scared."

It was a dare and Troy and Gina knew it. "Don't listen. You don't have to prove anything to him," she said.

"Maybe not, but if I caught one, it would sure shut him up."

"It's hard, Troy. To catch one, you have to move fast, and it's dangerous. You haven't even tried it before."

"No, but I'm a pretty good tree climber. This shouldn't be much different."

"But when you fall out of a tree, the ground isn't that far away."

"I never fall."

"Now you're sounding like Frank."

"What d'ya say?" yelled Frank.

"Where's the easiest spot to catch one?" Troy asked, quietly.

"If you're fast enough, it doesn't matter. Anywhere will do. Good luck."

Troy climbed along the metal beams until he reached Frank and the others. There was a large cluster of pigeons just a bit farther out. "Okay," pointed Frank. "Go for it."

For a few moments, Troy looked at the situation, trying to make a plan. Very slowly, he moved towards the pigeons, getting slower as he came closer. When he was almost close enough to reach out and catch one, he became very still as he stretched his hand towards them. When he was so close to one pigeon that he could hear it breathe, he simply reached out and grabbed it.

"Check it out," yelled Wally Westcott.

"Look at the size of it. I bet it's worth at least a buck fifty," shouted Billy Barton.

Tim Curly and Gina were equally amazed. "All right Troy. Yeah!" cheered Gina.

Troy was petting the pigeon as everyone but Frank shouted approval. Then, holding it in the air, he watched the wind grab the bird's feathers as he let it go.

"What are you, nuts?" yelled Frank.

"That bird was worth a lot of money," shouted Billy.

Troy thought hard for a moment. He wanted to tell them why he didn't kill the pigeon. It was because his kookum taught him that every animal was his brother, and that when you kill one, you had to pray for its spirit and use all of the animal. Its fur for clothing, its meat for food, bones for tools, every part of the animal could be used, and you had to use it. The animal is our brother, and deserves our respect. This is what he wanted to tell them, but he didn't. He didn't think Frank and his friends would understand. They would probably laugh. So instead, he said, "I wanted to show you I could catch it. I didn't want to kill it."

It didn't really matter to Frank that Troy let the pigeon go. What mattered was that Troy had caught one. "Now it's my turn to catch one," said Frank. Too impatient to try and catch one the way Troy did, he raced along the beams as fast as he could, but the pigeons were always a bit faster. After several minutes, he gave up and turned around. "I'll become the second person to ever reach the nesting beam, and the first to make it back without help."

"Forget it Frank," advised Billy. "It's too dangerous."

"Don't bother Frank, it's not that important," said Wally.

"Don't be an idiot," yelled Gina.

Troy watched with curiosity. "What's the nesting beam?"

"It's where the pigeons nest," Gina told him. "Only one of us has ever gone down there."

"Who's that?"

"Trent."

"I thought he was afraid of heights."

"That's why. He made it down, but he couldn't get back up and he stayed there all day hugging the beam. Firefighters finally got him out with a net."

Frank smiled and crawled quickly to the middle of the metal beams. He pointed below. When Troy looked down, he saw one large wooden beam stretching out under the tracks. Parts of it were broken away, but most of it was there. Troy couldn't tell how far down it was, but it looked far enough. Further down the nesting beam, near the huge stone pillars that supported the bridge, there were dozens of nests. "What do you say?" Frank taunted him. "We jump down, walk to the nests, and grab an armful of pigeons and their eggs."

"How do we get back?" Troy asked.

"We tie up the pigeons and the eggs in our shirts, throw them to Gina, then take a running start and jump up at the beam I'm standing on."

Troy looked down into the gulley. "You're crazy," he said.

"You and me," Frank continued. "Think you can? Do you have the guts? I do." Without another word, Frank climbed down and hanging from the metal beam, dropped himself straight down. Everyone gasped, then sighed in relief when he made a perfect landing on the nesting beam.

"You don't have to do this," Gina told Troy.

Troy bit his lip, then climbed down. Hanging above the nesting beam, he couldn't help thinking how small it looked. I can't do this, he thought to himself, Frank is a nut. About to pull himself back up, Troy felt the sweat on his fingers. It made his hands slip off the metal beam. In that moment, after he let go, Troy saw the distant downtown skyscrapers, then his kookum's face. He was floating, he felt weightless, but his stomach was still somewhere above him. And then, he hit the beam hard. He dropped to his knees, but stayed on. Frank was two feet away. He stared straight down into the gulley, too frightened to move.

"I made it," Troy whispered, "but I've never been more scared in my whole life. You're going to have to help me back up."

"Forget it," Frank said. "I'm not moving."

Troy could hear voices calling from above, but he just stared down at the distant rocks, praying the wind wouldn't blow too hard. "Say something," he finally heard Gina yelling.

"No," he and Frank said together. They still hadn't moved. Gina shook her head and turned to Tim.

"You better call the fire department."

Troy heard them but their voices were just murmurs. What he listened to as he crouched there was the water of the creek splashing against the rocks far below. He also heard his heartbeat. It seemed to pound within him and echo off the bridge. He wondered if the others could hear it too. His fingers were gripping the metal so tightly that they were going numb. He closed his eyes and he prayed.

Two hours later, after being lifted out from under the bridge by the firefighters, Troy and Frank stood at the end of Pigeon Street staring down. The ground had never looked more beautiful to either one of them. Gina stood beside them. "You guys are jerks."

Troy agreed, nodding his head. Frank grunted.

"How about a game of baseball?" Trent suggested.

"That sounds safe," Troy said. He could still feel his knees shaking. They wandered home to get their gloves.